King & Kayla

and the Case of the
Unhappy Neighbor

Written by
Dori Hillestad Butler

Illustrated by
Nancy Meyers

PEACHTREE
ATLANTA

For Kathy. I LOVE Kathy. She's my favorite editor.
—D. H. B.

To Quinn Marie and the great big incredibly smart
dog that your parents promise to get you some day
—N. M.

Ω

Published by
PEACHTREE PUBLISHING COMPANY INC.
1700 Chattahoochee Avenue
Atlanta, Georgia 30318-2112
www.peachtree-online.com

Text © 2020 by Dori Hillestad Butler
Illustrations © 2020 by Nancy Meyers

Edited by Kathy Landwehr
Design and composition by Nicola Simmonds Carmack
The illustrations were rendered in pencil, with color added digitally.

Printed in October 2019 by Toppan Leefung in China
10 9 8 7 6 5 4 3 2 1 (hardcover)
10 9 8 7 6 5 4 3 2 1 (trade paperback)
First Edition
HC ISBN 978-1-68263-055-6
PB ISBN 978-1-68263-056-3

Library of Congress Cataloging-in-Publication Data

Names: Butler, Dori Hillestad, author. | Meyers, Nancy, 1961– illustrator.
Title: King & Kayla and the case of the unhappy neighbor / written by Dori
Hillestad Butler ; illustrated by Nancy Meyers.
Other titles: King and Kayla and the case of the unhappy neighbor | Case of the
unhappy neighbor
Description: Atlanta : Peachtree Publishing Company Inc., [2020] | King the golden
retriever struggles to communicate with his human, Kayla, as both try to clear
Thor of having trashed Mr. Gary's yard.
Identifiers: LCCN 2018061618| ISBN 9781682630556 (hardcover) | ISBN
9781682630563 (trade pbk.)
Subjects: | CYAC: Mystery and detective stories. | Golden retriever—Fiction. |
Dogs—Fiction. | Neighbors—Fiction. | Orderliness—Fiction. | Human-animal
communication—Fiction.
Classification: LCC PZ7.B9759 Kiy 2020 | DDC [Fic]—dc23 LC record available at
https://lccn.loc.gov/2018061618

Contents

Chapter One

Trouble at Thor's House

Hello!

My name is King. I'm a dog. This is Kayla. She is my human.

Kayla and I are on a walk. I LOVE walks. They're my favorite thing!

"Good morning, Mouse!" I say.

"GOOD MORNING, KING," Mouse says. Mouse is a BIG dog with a BIG voice.

"Hi, Thor! Hello, Jillian!" I say.

Jillian is Thor's human.

"Hi, King!" Thor says.

Uh oh…I smell trouble at
Thor's house.

So does Kayla.

"What's the matter, Jillian?" Kayla asks.

"Everyone's mad at Thor," Jillian says.

"Why?" Kayla asks.

"He's been digging again," Jillian
says. "Last night he dug a hole and
escaped from our yard."

"I'm a good dog!" Thor says.

"Good dogs don't eat other dogs'
ears," I say.

"We didn't know Thor was loose until Mr. Gary called and told us," Jillian tells Kayla.

Gulp! I know that guy. He gets mad if you put a paw on his yard.

"Oh no. Was Thor in Mr. Gary's yard?" Kayla asks.

Jillian nods. "He dug up the garden and got into the trash. My mom is helping Mr. Gary clean up the mess."

"I didn't make a mess," Thor says.
"All I did was chase Cat with No Name
 away!"

"Hm," I say.

"It'll be okay," Kayla tells Jillian.
"Thor is still a puppy. He'll settle down
 when he gets bigger."

"I hope so," Jillian says.

Chapter Two
A New Guy

On our way home, we stop by Mr. Gary's house to check things out.

There's a big mess all right. But it doesn't look like the kind of mess Thor would make.

Kayla doesn't think so either.

"Are you sure Thor did all this?" she asks Jillian's mom. "Does he—"

Mr. Gary doesn't let her finish her question. "I saw him in my yard," he says.

"And we know he likes to dig," Jillian's mom says.

"Please move along," Mr. Gary says.
"I don't want your dog to do his
business on my yard."

I wouldn't do my business on his yard.
I don't like the way it smells.

"Come on, King," Kayla says. "Let's
go back to Jillian's house. I have
some questions for her."

On the way, we pass Cat with No Name. He doesn't have a name because he doesn't have people.

Wait a minute. If he doesn't have people, how does he get food? I wonder…

"Hey, Cat! Did you steal food from Mr. Gary's garden?" I ask.

"No. The new guy did," says Cat.

"What new guy?" I ask. "I didn't know there was a new guy in the neighborhood."

"Watch out for him," Cat says. "He'll fight you."

GULP!

Chapter Three
Kayla's Questions

"Yay! You're back!" Thor says.

"I saw partly eaten tomatoes, strawberries, and carrots all over Mr. Gary's yard," Kayla tells Jillian. "Does Thor like tomatoes, strawberries, and carrots?"

I LOVE tomatoes, strawberries, and carrots. They're my favorite foods!

"I don't know," Jillian says.

"Let's find out," Kayla says.

Jillian goes inside her house.
She comes back with a tomato, a
strawberry, and a carrot.

Thor sniffs them all,
then runs away.

"I don't think he likes
any of those things,"
Jillian says.

"I have another question," Kayla says.

"Is Thor strong enough to knock over a
heavy trash can?"

"Let's find out," Jillian says.

We go to the trash cans.

"Come on, Thor. Knock it over!"
Jillian says.

Thor leaps against the trash can.

It doesn't fall over.

"Thor didn't do it! He didn't mess up
Mr. Gary's yard!" Jillian says.

"I'm a good dog!" Thor cries.

"So if Thor didn't do it, who did?"
Kayla asks.

She takes out her notebook and pencil.

"Let's make a list of everything we know about this case."

1. Someone messed up Mr. Gary's yard.

2. Mr. Gary saw Thor in his yard last night.

3. Thor doesn't like tomatoes, strawberries, or carrots.

4. Thor isn't big enough to knock over a heavy trash can.

If I could write, I would add this to
Kayla's list of things we know:

"Now, let's make a list of what we don't know about this case," Kayla says.

1. Who likes tomatoes, strawberries, and carrots?

2. Who is big enough to knock over a heavy trash can?

3. Who else was in Mr. Gary's yard?

If I could write, I would add this to

Kayla's list of things we don't know:

Who is the new guy?
Is he dangerous?

"Now we need a plan," Kayla says.

I have a plan:

Find the new guy!

Chapter Four
Spread Out and Sniff!

Look! Jillian's gate is open. We can search for the new guy right now.

But what if Cat with No Name is right about him? What if he wants to fight me?

"WHERE ARE YOU GOING, KING?" Mouse asks.

I tell Mouse all about our case.

Then I ask, "Do you
know the new guy?"

"NO," Mouse says.
"HOW DO WE FIND
HIM?"

"If he was in Mr. Gary's yard, we should be able to find his scent and track him," I say.

"LET'S GO," Mouse says. He jumps his fence.

"Wait for me!" Thor cries.

We run down the street.

"Hey!" Mouse's human yells. "All of our dogs are loose!"

"King! Thor! Come back here!" Kayla and Jillian yell.

"Sorry. We're busy," I tell Kayla.

"Yeah, we're busy!" Thor says.

Kayla, Jillian, and Mouse's human chase us down the street.

"Oh, no," Jillian moans.

"Not Mr. Gary's yard again."

"Spread out and sniff!" I tell Mouse
and Thor.

"I THINK I'VE GOT THE NEW
GUY'S SCENT," Mouse says.

"Me too," I say. "And guess what?
I don't think the new guy is a dog!"

"Aha! Look what I found," I say.
"I'm pretty sure it came from the
new guy."

Oh, boy! I LOVE books.
They're my favorite things!

"...a great introduction to mysteries, gathering facts, and analytical thinking for an unusually young set."
—*Booklist*

"A perfect option for newly independent readers ready to start transitioning from easy readers to beginning chapter books."—*School Library Journal*

"Readers will connect with this charmingly misunderstood pup (along with his exasperated howls, excited tail wagging, and sheepish grins)." —*Kirkus Reviews*

King & Kayla and the Case of the Missing Dog Treats
HC: 978-1-56145-877-6
PB: 978-1-68263-015-0

King & Kayla and the Case of the Mysterious Mouse
HC: 978-1-56145-879-0
PB: 978-1-68263-017-4

King & Kayla and the Case of the Secret Code
HC: 978-1-56145-878-3
PB: 978-1-68263-016-7

King & Kayla and the Case of the Lost Tooth
HC: 978-1-56145-880-6
PB: 978-1-68263-018-1

King & Kayla and the Case of Found Fred
HC: 978-1-68263-052-5
PB: 978-1-68263-053-2

"I told you I'm a good dog!" Thor says.

We are all good dogs. And good friends!

The End

Mr. Gary runs over. You can almost
see smoke coming out of his ears.

"WHO DID THIS? WHO
POOPED IN MY YARD?"
he yells at Mouse, Thor,
and me.

"None of them," Kayla says.

"How do you know?" Mr. Gary asks.

"Because that's not dog poop,"
Kayla says.

No, it's not.

Chapter Five
A New Word

Mouse's human takes out his phone.

"What are you doing?" Kayla asks.

"I'm looking for a scat chart," Mouse's human says.

"What's scat?" Jillian asks.

Kayla whispers, "It's another word for poop."

"Let's see if we can figure out what kind of animal left that scat," Mouse's human says.

The humans all look at the chart.
Then they look at the scat.

I don't need to see the chart. I can
smell who left the scat.

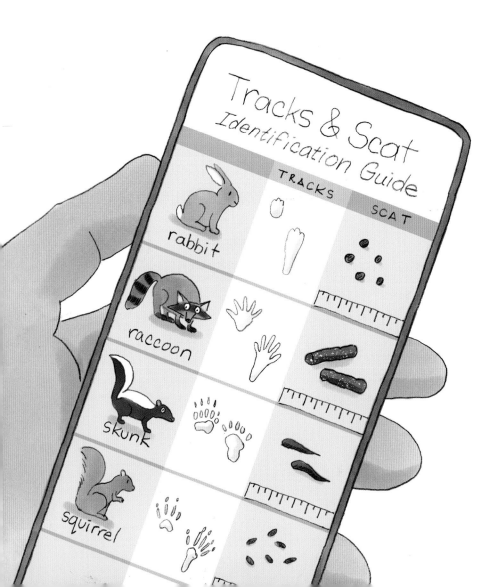

"A raccoon!" Kayla and Jillian say at the same time.

That's right.

"Raccoons get into the trash," Jillian says.

"They dig up gardens, too," Kayla says.

Mr. Gary turns to Jillian. "Perhaps I was wrong to accuse your dog of messing up my yard."

"I'm glad you let us know he was loose," Jillian says.